Dalmatian Press, 1999

The Fastex Racing Team has been waiting months to test their driving skills against Rexcor. With the first race less than a week away and members of the Rexcor Team scheming behind their backs, Flyer, Megan, Stunts, and Charger have been spending extra time on the practice tracks.

"I can't wait to show The Collector what real racing is like after that trick he pulled on Charger the other night at the diner," said Stunts.

"Me too," said Megan, "but we have to be careful against those guys. You never know what tricks they may have up their sleeves. This race is really important to Team Fastex and my dad."

Megan's dad, Jack Fassler, is the owner of the Fastex Racing Team and developer of New Motor City. This first race was more important to him than Megan realizes. His long-time rival and Rexcor Team owner, Garner Rexton, had purchased the bank that had given Jack a huge loan. Now, Garner was making it as hard as possible on Jack. Jack needed this victory money to pay off the loan, or the team and the MotorSphere would be taken away.

While Megan briefed the team on safety adjustments made to the race cars, Garner was doing his own briefing back at Rexcor Headquarters.

"Team Fastex is your enemy," he told his racers. "We cannot allow them to win this first race. I will give each of you a one million dollar bonus if Team Rexcor wins."

"No problem, boss-man," said Zorina. "After the other night, I am sure we have them shaking in their racing suits."

Garner interrupted, "Well just in case, Spex is waiting for you in the garage with a little 'insurance.'"

Spex was the crew chief for Rexcor. Part man, but mostly machine, Spex was an intimidating member of the team.

"This is a special chip to be placed in the engine of a Fastex car. It will cause an engine to overheat and will not allow the car to shut off," Spex said slowly. "And when the car gets too hot, it will be completely destroyed!"

"I know just the car for this little wonder chip," said The Collector, as he and Junker headed out the door.

Raceday finally arrived. The streets were jammed with traffic and the fans were lined up, ready for action. The MotorSphere was everything they had hoped for, an entire racing world under one roof.

The racing teams waited nervously in the pit garages. Mechanics changed tires, while other crew members prepared the mobile pit units. Soon it was time for the race to begin.

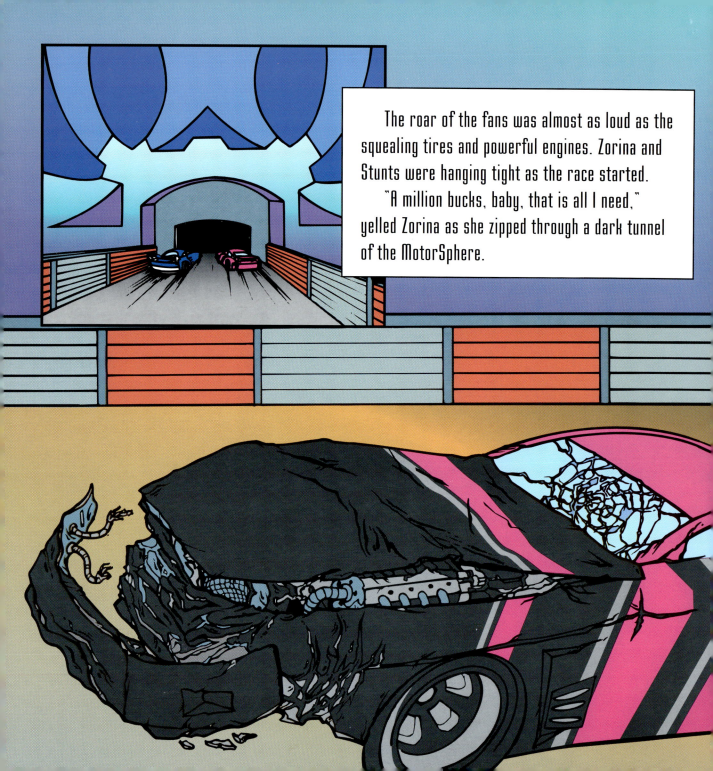

The roar of the fans was almost as loud as the squealing tires and powerful engines. Zorina and Stunts were hanging tight as the race started.

"A million bucks, baby, that is all I need," yelled Zorina as she zipped through a dark tunnel of the MotorSphere.

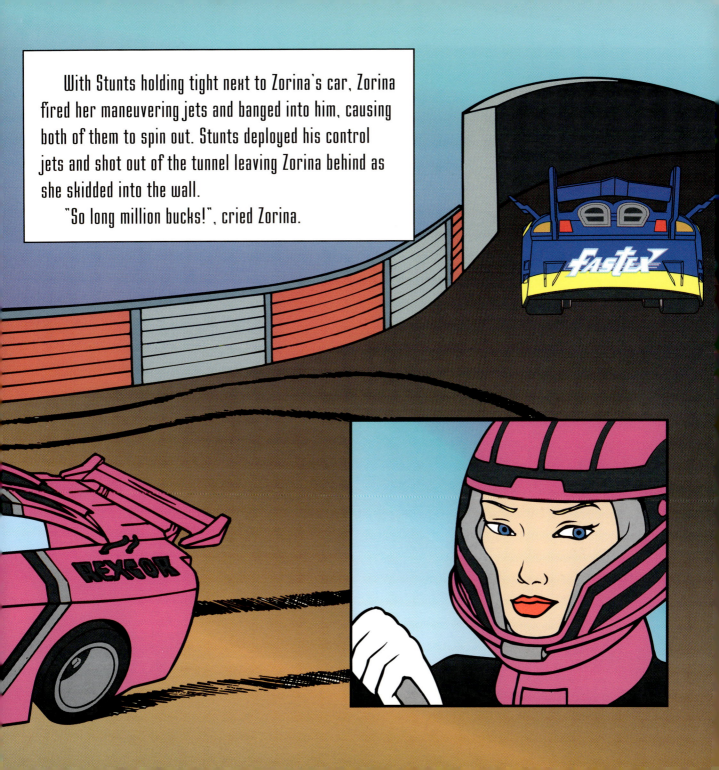

With Stunts holding tight next to Zorina's car, Zorina fired her maneuvering jets and banged into him, causing both of them to spin out. Stunts deployed his control jets and shot out of the tunnel leaving Zorina behind as she skidded into the wall.

"So long million bucks!", cried Zorina.

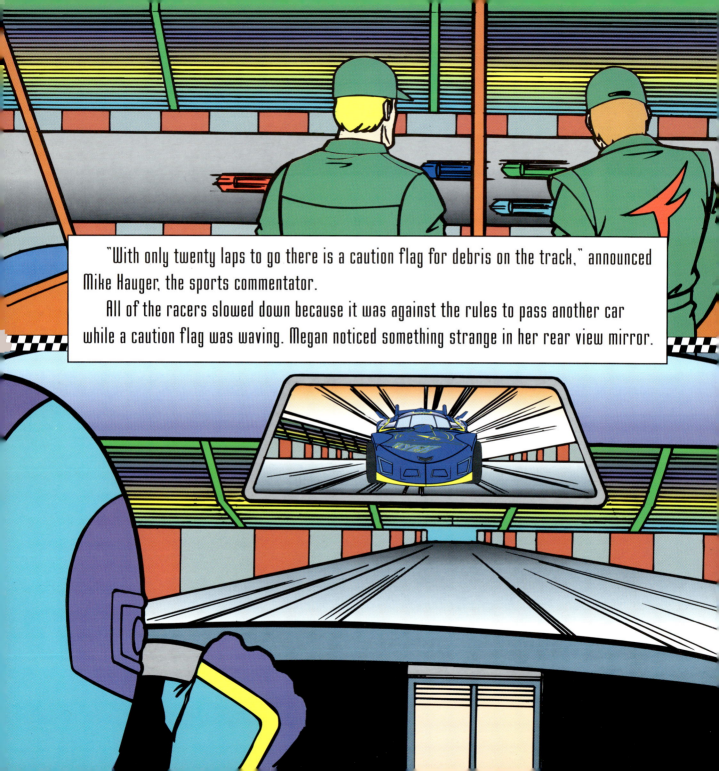

"With only twenty laps to go there is a caution flag for debris on the track," announced Mike Hauger, the sports commentator.

All of the racers slowed down because it was against the rules to pass another car while a caution flag was waving. Megan noticed something strange in her rear view mirror.

Jack and Duck, the crew chief, quickly got on the radio to help Flyer.

"Flyer, this is Jack. Listen carefully. You cannot stop or slow down, the engine will blow up. And you do not have time to let your fuel run out because the heat will reach critical and cause a huge explosion that could endanger everyone!"

It looked as if Garner Rexton's evil plan was going to work. But, Flyer had an idea. "I'll take it to the river and use my rescue racer to escape."

Megan broke in on the radio, "I'm following him, Dad. He'll need my help."

Jack lowered his head, knowing Megan would be in danger, too.

Megan followed Flyer off the track as he headed toward the city. Just before Flyer left the MotorSphere, Junker launched his grappling hook and caught Flyer's rear bumper. Flyer did not let it stop him. Flyer deployed his wings and as he got in the air, he dropped Junker into a garbage truck!

"You have five minutes to get to the river or you'll never make it!" cried Megan. Flyer understood what he had to do. Weaving in and out of traffic, smashing fire hydrants, and flying over buildings, the teammates headed for the river. With flames already surrounding the car's engine, Flyer could feel the clock ticking.

Flyer crashed through a wooden fence that blocked a cliff.

"You have to get out!" cried Megan.

Flyer launched his rescue racer. The car headed over the cliff in a ball of fire. Flyer struggled to stop his escape vehicle.

Megan shot her grappling hook, attaching it to Flyer's rescue racer's bumper. The line on the hook snapped tight as the escape pod went over the edge.

But the bumper slipped from the line. Quickly, Flyer climbed out and and grabbed the line just as the rescue racer fell to the river. Megan and Flyer were safe. Garner's plan had failed.

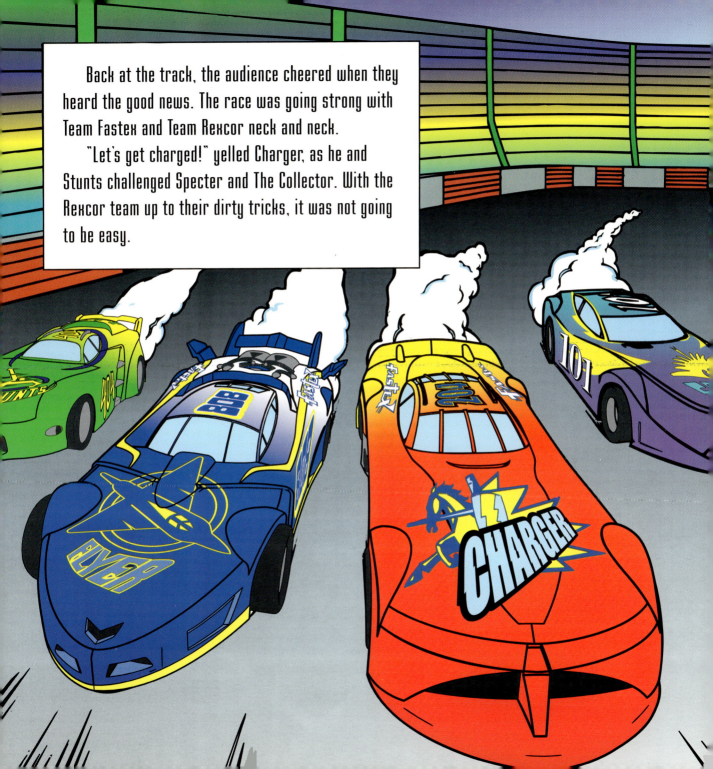

Back at the track, the audience cheered when they heard the good news. The race was going strong with Team Fastex and Team Rexcor neck and neck.

"Let's get charged!" yelled Charger, as he and Stunts challenged Specter and The Collector. With the Rexcor team up to their dirty tricks, it was not going to be easy.

The cars bumped and banged into each other. Everyone used their special jets and driving skills to try to get ahead. Specter hit the wall and his race was finished.

Stunts drove his car up on two wheels to keep The Collector from crashing into Charger. Stunts' car flipped and bumped into The Collector whose car filled with impact foam. Stunts was out of the race, but he was safe.

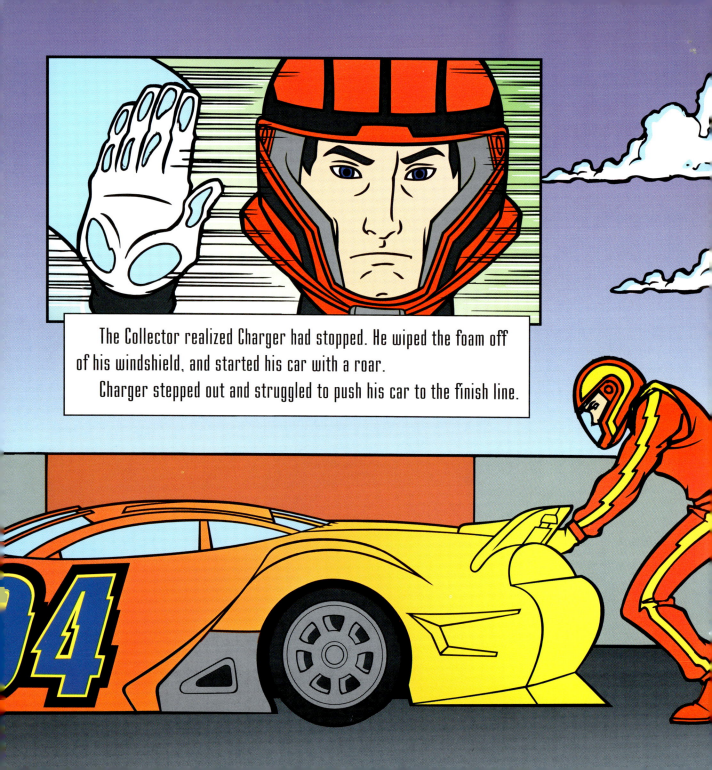

The Collector realized Charger had stopped. He wiped the foam off of his windshield, and started his car with a roar.

Charger stepped out and struggled to push his car to the finish line.

The crowd cheered, "PUSH, PUSH, PUSH..."
Charger heard The Collector close behind him. With a burst of energy,
Charger pushed his car over the finish line and the checkered flag came down.

Jack ran to the track. "You did it! You saved the Fastex Racing Team!"

"No, we saved the team," said Charger, as the four drivers gave high-fives.

Once again, Team Fastex were the heroes of the race track.